When I Grow Bigger

For Kieron, Natalie, Leanne and Sam
"Oh, to see everything through your eyes,
surprise after surprise after SURPRISE!"
T.C.

For little Camelia and Angelica
and Tiziana
J.B-B.

First published 1994 by Walker Books Ltd
87 Vauxhall Walk, London SE11 5HJ

2 4 6 8 10 9 7 5 3 1

Text © 1994 Trish Cooke
Illustrations © 1994 John Bendall-Brunello

This book has been typeset in Sabon.

Printed in Italy

British Library Cataloguing in Publication Data
A catalogue record for this book
is available from the British Library.
ISBN 0-7445-2505-5

When I Grow Bigger

written by

TRISH COOKE

illustrated by

JOHN BENDALL-BRUNELLO

WALKER BOOKS
LONDON

"When I grow bigger,
I'm going to reach
up, up, up
to the ceiling,"
said Leanne.

"When I grow bigger,
I'm going to reach
up, up, up
to the clouds,"
said Sam.

"When I grow bigger,
I'm going to reach
up, up, up
to the sky,"
said Natalie.

Thomas looked
up at them,
like three tall towers
they were…

and they looked
down at him
and laughed...

"You're just a baby," said Natalie, patting Thomas on the head.

"You're just a nipper," said Sam, bending down to look at Thomas.

"You're just a little 'un," said Leanne, trying to pick Thomas up.

But Thomas wriggled and squirmed until he got free.
Leave me alone, Thomas thought.
But the words didn't come out, just YAAGHs and YELLs.

And that's what they did,
they left Thomas alone,
all alone sitting by
Thomas's dad's daffodils.

And THEY,
the three BIG people,
went off to play in
Thomas's dad's
wheelbarrow.

"You get in,"
said Natalie.

"I want to push,"
said Natalie.

"Let me,"
said Sam.

Thomas watched THEM,
the three BIG people,
quarrelling.

Thomas watched
THEM,
the three BIG people,
fighting.

"Ow!" said Natalie.
"You!" said Sam.

"I'm telling!"
said Leanne,
running towards
the house.

Along came Thomas's dad's feet.
Thomas didn't look up but
he knew they were Dad's feet
because he had green wellies on.
(Mum's are red!)
Dad's green wellies
stopped by the daffodils.
He nearly tripped
over Thomas.

"Oooops! Didn't
see you there!"
said Dad.

Thomas was not happy.
Then Dad stooped down
to pick Thomas up.
But Thomas wriggled
and squirmed
and tried
to get free.

"Hey, what's up?"
said Dad.

And then Leanne yelled,
"THEY'RE FIGHTING!"

So Thomas's dad
held on tight
to Thomas
and ran.

"He started it," said Natalie.

"No, I didn't," said Sam.

Leanne caught up and huffed and puffed.

"OK, OK," said Thomas's dad. "I don't want to know, just play properly, all of you!"

Thomas's dad put Thomas
in the wheelbarrow.
Natalie and Sam
took the handles
and Leanne
looked cross.

"There's nothing to do,"
Leanne said.

"Mmmmmmmmm,"
said Natalie.

And Sam sat down.

Thomas looked
over the side of
the wheelbarrow.
It was a long
way down.

"The baby wants to get out," said Natalie.

"OK, OK," said Sam.

"I'll do it," said Leanne.

Thomas's dad looked over, so Natalie helped Leanne get Thomas out. Sam held the handles of Thomas's dad's wheelbarrow.

"No, I will," said Natalie.

"I wish you would hurry up and grow big," said Leanne.

"Yes, I wish you'd hurry up!" said Sam.

Natalie shook her head. "Ah, he's just a baby," she said.

"Humph," moaned Leanne.

"What shall we do now?"
yawned Sam.

"I don't know,"
said Natalie.

"I know,"
said Leanne.

And she started to go
towards the house.
Thomas's dad
was watching,
so Natalie and Sam
held Thomas's hand.

"Come on,"
said Sam.

"Hurry up,"
whispered Leanne.

Natalie sighed.
"What are we
doing now?"

"We're going to do something," said Leanne.

"What?" asked Sam.

"Yes, what?" said Natalie.

"MAKE THOMAS GROW!" Leanne said.

"YAAAGH!"

cried Thomas.

Dad stopped and smiled.
"What are you up to?"
Thomas's dad said.

"Nothing,"
said Natalie,

"Nothing,"
said Sam,

"Nothing,"
said Leanne,

and they
went inside.

"I'll hold his hands,"
said Leanne.

"What about me?"
said Natalie.

"I'll hold his feet,"
said Sam.

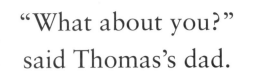

"What about you?"
said Thomas's dad.

"We're only playing,"
said Natalie
and Sam
and Leanne.

Thomas put his
arms up to Dad.

Dad picked him up. Thomas was almost as high as the ceiling!

And then Thomas's dad went outside. Thomas was almost as high as the clouds.

Thomas's hands were up in the air, almost as high as the sky. And Thomas was laughing!

Natalie and Sam and
Leanne watched.

"When I grow bigger…"
said Leanne,

"Oh, be quiet,"
said Sam,

"Yes, be quiet,"
said Natalie,

looking up, up, up
at BIG Thomas
having fun!